ODD

and the

FROST
GIANTS

ODD

and the

FROST
GIANTS

———————

NEIL GAIMAN

Illustrated by
BRETT HELQUIST

HARPER

An Imprint of HarperCollinsPublishers

Odd and the Frost Giants
Text copyright © 2009 by Neil Gaiman
Illustrations copyright © 2009 by Brett Helquist

Library of Congress Cataloging-in-Publication Data
Gaiman, Neil.
    Odd and the Frost Giants / Neil Gaiman ; illustrated by Brett
Helquist. — 1st ed.
        p.   cm.
    Summary: An unlucky twelve-year-old Norwegian boy named Odd
leads the Norse gods Loki, Thor, and Odin in an attempt to outwit evil
Frost Giants who have taken over Asgard.
    ISBN 978-0-06-167173-9 (trade bdg.)
    [1. Heroes—Fiction.   2. Loki (Norse deity)—Fiction.   3. Thor
(Norse deity)—Fiction.   4. Odin (Norse deity)—Fiction.   5. Giants—
Fiction.   6. Mythology, Norse—Fiction.]   I. Helquist, Brett, ill.
II. Title.
PZ7.G1273Odd   2009   2009014574
[Fic]—dc22   CIP
                                                                 AC

Typography by Hilary Zarycky
09 10 11 12 13   LP/RRDC   10 9 8 7 6 5 4 3 2 1
❖

First Edition

For Iselin and Linnea

CONTENTS

———·•·———

ODD

and the

FROST
GIANTS

CHAPTER 1

ODD

THERE WAS A BOY called Odd, and there was
nothing strange or unusual about that, not in
that time or place. Odd meant *the tip of a blade*,
and it was a lucky name.

He *was* odd, though. At least, the other villagers thought so. But if there was one thing that he
wasn't, it was lucky.

His father had been killed during a sea raid

two years before, when Odd was ten. It was not unknown for people to get killed in sea raids, but his father wasn't killed by a Scotsman, dying in glory in the heat of battle as a Viking should. He had jumped overboard to rescue one of the stocky little ponies that they took with them on their raids as pack animals.

They would load the ponies up with all the gold and valuables and food and weapons that they could find, and the ponies would trudge back to the longship. The ponies were the most valuable and hardworking things on the ship. After Olaf the Tall was killed by a Scotsman, Odd's father had to look after the ponies. Odd's father wasn't very experienced with ponies, being a woodcutter and wood-carver by trade, but he did his best. On the return journey, one of the ponies got loose during a squall off Orkney and fell overboard.

Odd's father jumped into the grey sea with a rope, pulled the pony back to the ship and, with the other Vikings, hauled it back up on deck.

He died before the next morning of the cold and the wet and the water in his lungs.

When they returned to Norway, they told Odd's mother, and Odd's mother told Odd. Odd just shrugged. He didn't cry. He didn't say anything.

Nobody knew what Odd was feeling on the inside. Nobody knew what he thought. And, in a village on the banks of a fjord, where everybody knew everybody's business, that was infuriating.

There were no full-time Vikings back then. Everybody had another job. Sea raiding was something the men did for fun or to get things they couldn't find in their village. They even got their wives that way. Odd's mother, who was as dark as Odd's father had been fair, had been brought to

3

the fjord on a longship from Scotland. She would sing Odd the ballads that she had learned as a girl, back before Odd's father had taken her knife away and thrown her over his shoulder and carried her back to the longship.

Odd wondered if she missed Scotland, but when he asked her, she said no, not really, she just missed people who spoke her language. She could speak the language of the Norse now, but with an accent.

Odd's father had been a master of the axe. He had a one-room cabin that he had built from logs deep in the little forest behind the fjord, and he would go out to the woods and return a week or so later with his handcart piled high with logs, all ready to weather and to split, for they made everything they could out of wood in those parts: wooden nails joined wooden boards to build

4

wooden dwellings or wooden boats. In the winter, when the snows were too deep for travel, Odd's father would sit by the fire and carve, making wood into faces and toys and drinking cups and bowls, while Odd's mother sewed and cooked and, always, sang.

She had a beautiful voice.

Odd didn't understand the words of the songs she sang, but she would translate them after she had sung them, and his head would roil with fine lords riding out on their great horses, their noble falcons on their wrists, brave hounds always padding by their sides, off to get into all manner of trouble, fighting giants and rescuing maidens and freeing the oppressed from tyranny.

After Odd's father died, his mother sang less and less.

Odd kept smiling, though, and it drove the

Odd's father would sit by the fire and carve, making wood
into faces and toys and drinking cups and bowls.

villagers mad. He even smiled after the accident that crippled his right leg.

It was three weeks after the longship had come back without his father's body. Odd had taken his father's tree-cutting axe, so huge he could hardly lift it, and had hauled it out into the woods, certain that he knew all there was to know about cutting trees and determined to put this knowledge into practice.

He should possibly, he admitted to his mother later, have used the smaller axe and a smaller tree to practise on.

Still, what he did was remarkable.

After the tree had fallen on his foot, he had used the axe to dig away the earth beneath his leg and he had pulled it out, and he had cut a branch to make himself a crutch to lean on, for the bones in his leg were shattered. And, somehow, he had got himself home, hauling his father's heavy axe with him, for metal was rare in those hills and axes needed to be bartered or stolen, and he could not have left it to rust.

So two years passed, and Odd's mother married Fat Elfred, who was amiable enough when he had not been drinking, but he already had four sons and three daughters from a previous marriage (his wife had been struck by lightning), and he had no time for a crippled stepson, so Odd spent more and more time out in the great woods.

Odd loved the spring, when the waterfalls began to course down the valleys and the woodland was covered with flowers. He liked summer, when the first berries began to ripen, and autumn, when there were nuts and small apples. Odd did not care for the winter, when the villagers spent as much time as they could in the village's great hall, eating root vegetables and salted meat. In winter the men would fight and fart and sing and sleep and wake and fight again, and the women would shake their heads and sew and knit and mend.

By March, the worst of the winter would be over. The snow would thaw, the rivers begin to run and the world would wake into itself again.

Not that year.

Winter hung in there, like an invalid refusing to die. Day after grey day the ice stayed hard; the world remained unfriendly and cold.

In the village, people got on one another's nerves. They'd been staring at each other across the great hall for four months now. It was time for the men to make the longship seaworthy, time for the women to start clearing the ground for planting. The games became nasty. The jokes became mean. Fights were to hurt.

Which is why, one morning at the end of March—some hours before the sun was up, when the frost was hard and the ground still like iron, while Fat Elfred and his children and Odd's mother were still asleep—Odd put on his thickest, warmest clothes, stole a side of smoke-blackened salmon from where it hung in the rafters of Fat Elfred's house and a firepot with a handful of glowing embers from the fire; and he took his father's second-best axe, which he tied by a leather thong to his belt, and limped out into the woods.

The snow was deep and treacherous, with a thick, shiny crust of ice. It would have been hard walking for a man with two good legs, but for a boy with one good leg, one very bad leg and a wooden crutch, every hill was a mountain.

Odd crossed a frozen lake, which should have melted weeks before, and went deep into the woods. The days seemed almost as short as they had been in midwinter, and although it was only midafternoon it was dark as night by the time he reached his father's old woodcutting hut.

The door was blocked by snow, and Odd had to take a wooden spade and dig it out before he could enter. He fed the firepot with kindling, and tended it until he felt safe transferring the fire into the fireplace, where the old logs were dry.

On the floor he found a lump of wood, slightly bigger than his fist. He was going to throw it on the fire, but his fingers felt carving on the small wooden block, and so he put it to one side, to look at when it was light. He gathered snow in a small pan, and melted it over the fire, and he ate smoked fish and hot berry-water.

It was good. There were blankets in the corner still, and a straw-stuffed mattress, and he could imagine that the little room smelled of his father, and nobody hit him or called him a cripple or an idiot, and so, after building the fire high enough that it would still be burning in the morning, he went to sleep quite happy.

CHAPTER 2

THE FOX, THE EAGLE AND THE BEAR

ODD WAS WOKEN BY something scratching against the hut. He pulled himself up to his feet, thought briefly about tales of trolls and monsters, hoped that it wasn't a bear, then opened the door. It was daylight outside, which meant it was late in the morning, and a fox was staring up at him, insolently, from the snow.

Its muzzle was narrow, its ears were pricked

and sharp and its expression was calculating and sly. When it saw that Odd was watching, it jumped into the air, as if it were trying to show off, and retreated a little way and then stopped. It was red-orange, like flame, and it took a dancing step or two towards Odd, and turned away, then looked back at Odd as if it were inviting him to follow.

It was, Odd concluded, an animal with a plan. He had no plans, other than a general determination never to return to the village. And it was not every day that you got to follow a fox.

So he did.

It moved like a flame, always ahead of him. If Odd slowed down, if the terrain was too difficult, if the boy got tired, then the fox would simply wait patiently at the top of the nearest rise until Odd was ready, and then its tail would go up, and it would flicker forward into the snow.

Odd pressed on.

There was a bird circling high overhead. *A hawk*, Odd thought, and then it landed in a dead tree, and he realized how big it was and knew it was an eagle. Its head was cocked oddly to one side, and Odd was convinced it was watching him.

He followed the fox up a hill and down another (down was harder than up for Odd, in the snow, with one bad foot and a crutch, and several times he fell) and then halfway up another, to a place where a dead pine tree stuck out from the hill like a rotten tooth. A silver birch tree grew close beside the dead pine. And it was here that the fox stopped.

A mournful bellow greeted them.

The dead tree had a hole in one side, the kind

15

that bees sometimes inhabit and fill with honey-comb. The people in Odd's village would make the honey into the alcoholic mead they drank to celebrate the safe return of their Vikings, and the midwinter, and any other excuse they needed to celebrate.

An enormous brown bear had its front paw caught in the hollow of the pine tree.

Odd smiled grimly. It was obvious what had happened.

In order to get at the pine tree hollow, the bear had leaned its weight against the birch tree, bending it down and moving it out of the way. But the moment the bear had pushed its paw into the hole, it had taken its weight off the birch, which had snapped back, and now the bear was pro-foundly trapped.

The animal bellowed once more, a deeply

An enormous brown bear had its front paw
caught in the hollow of the pine tree.

grumpy bellow. It looked miserable, but not as if it were about to attack.

Warily Odd walked towards the tree.

Above them, the eagle circled.

Odd unhooked his axe from his belt and walked around the pine tree. He cut a piece of wood about six inches long and used it to prop the two trees apart; he did not want to crush the bear's paw. Then, with clean, economical blows, he swung the blade of his axe against the birch. The wood was hard, but he kept swinging, and he had soon come close to cutting it through.

Odd looked at the bear. The bear looked at Odd with big brown eyes. Odd spoke aloud. "I can't run," he said to the bear. "So if you want to eat me, you'll find me easy prey. But I should have worried about that before, shouldn't I? Too late now."

He took a deep breath and swung the axe one last time. The birch tree tipped and fell away from the bear, who blinked and pulled its paw from the hollow in the pine tree. The paw was dripping with honey.

The bear licked its paw with a startlingly pink tongue. Odd, who was hungry, picked a lump of honeycomb from the edge of the hole, and ate it, wax and all. The honey oozed down his throat and made him cough.

The bear made a snuffling noise. It reached into the tree, pulled out a huge lump of comb and finished it off in a couple of bites. Then it stood up on its hind legs and it roared.

Odd wondered if he was going to die now, if the honey had just been an appetizer, but the bear got down on all fours once more and continued, single-mindedly, to empty the tree of honey.

It was getting dark.

Odd knew it was time for him to head for home. He started down the hill, and was almost at the bottom when he realized that he had absolutely no idea where his hut was. He had followed the fox to get here, but the fox was not going to lead him back. He tried to hurry, and he stumbled on a patch of ice, and his crutch went flying. He landed face-first in the hard snow.

He crawled towards his crutch, and as he did so, he felt hot breath on the back of his neck.

"Hello, bear," said Odd, cheerfully. "You had better eat me. I'll be more use as bear food than I will be frozen to death on the ice."

The bear did not seem to want to eat Odd. It sat down on the ice in front of him, and gestured with its paw.

"You mean it?" said Odd. "You aren't going to eat me?"

The bear made a rumbling sort of noise in the back of its throat. But it was a gloomy noise, and not a hungry noise, and Odd decided to chance his luck. The day could not get stranger, after all.

He clambered onto the bear's back, holding his crutch with his left hand and clutching the bear's fur with his right. The bear stood up slowly, making sure the boy was on, then set off at a fast lope through the twilight.

As the bear sped up, the cold went through Odd's clothes and chilled him to the bone.

The fox dashed ahead of them, the eagle flew above them and Odd thought crazily, happily, *I'm just like one of the brave lords in my mother's ballads. Only without the horse, the dog and the falcon.*

And he thought, *I can never tell anyone about this, because they won't believe it. Because even I wouldn't believe it.*

Snow fell from branches as they brushed past and stung his face, but he laughed as they went. The moon rose, pale and huge, and cold, cold, but Odd laughed some more, because his hut was waiting for him, and he was an impossible lord riding a bear, and because he was Odd.

The bear stopped in front of Odd's hut, and Odd half climbed, half fell from the beast's back. He pulled himself up with his crutch, and then he said, "Thank you." He thought the bear nodded its head in the moonlight, but perhaps he imagined it.

There was a crash of wings, and the eagle landed on the snow a few feet from Odd. It tipped its head on one side to stare at Odd with an eye the color of honey. There was nothing but darkness where its other eye should have been.

He walked up to his door. The fox was already

waiting there, sitting like a dog. The bear padded up to the hut behind him.

Odd looked from one animal to the other. "What?" he said testily, although it was obvious what they wanted.

And then, "I suppose you had better come in," he said. He opened the door.

And they came in.

CHAPTER 3

THE NIGHT CONVERSATION

ODD HAD IMAGINED THAT the side of salmon would feed him for a week or more. But bears and foxes and eagles all, he discovered, eat salmon, and he felt that feeding them was the least he could do to thank them for seeing him home. They ate until it was all gone, but only Odd and the eagle seemed satisfied. The fox and the bear both looked like they were still hungry.

"We'll find more food tomorrow," said Odd. "Sleep now."

The animals stared at him. He walked over to the straw mattress and climbed onto it, placing the crutch carefully against the wall, to pull himself up with when he woke. The bed didn't smell like his father at all, he realized, as he lay down. It just smelled like straw. Odd closed his eyes, and he was asleep.

Dreams of darkness, of flashes, of moments—nothing he could hold on to, nothing that comforted him. And then into the dream came a booming gloomy voice that said, "It wasn't my fault."

A higher voice, bitterly amused, said, "Oh, right. I *told* you not to go pushing that tree down. You just didn't listen."

"I was hungry. I could smell the honey. You

don't know what it was like, smelling that honey.
It was better than mead. Better than roasted
goose." And then, the gloomy voice, so bass
it made Odd's stomach vibrate, changed its
tone. "And *you*, of all people, don't need to go
blaming anyone else. It's because of you we're
in this mess."

"I thought we had a deal. I thought we weren't
going to keep harping on about a trivial little mis-
take . . ."

"You call this trivial?"

And then a third voice, high and raw, screeched,
"Silence."

There was silence. Odd rolled over. There was
a glow from the fire embers, enough to see the
inside of the hut, enough to confirm to Odd that
there were not another three people in there with
him. It was just him and the fox and the bear and
the eagle . . .

"It's because of you we're in this mess."

Whatever they are, thought Odd, *they don't seem to eat people.*

He sat up, leaned against the wall. The bear and the eagle both ignored him. The fox darted him a green-eyed glance.

"You were talking," said Odd.

The animals looked at Odd and at one another. If they did not actually say "Who? Us?" it was there in their expressions, in the way they held themselves.

"*Somebody* was talking," said Odd, "and it wasn't me. There isn't anyone else in here. That means it was you lot. And there's no point in arguing."

"We weren't arguing," said the bear. "Because we can't talk." Then it said, "Oops."

The fox and the eagle glared at the bear, who put a paw over its eyes and looked ashamed of itself.

Odd sighed. "Which one of you wants to explain what's going on?" he said.

"Nothing's going on," said the fox brightly. "Just a few talking animals. Nothing to worry about. Happens every day. We'll be out of your hair first thing in the morning."

The eagle fixed Odd with its one good eye. Then it turned to the fox. "Tell!"

The fox shifted uncomfortably. "Why me?"

"Oh," said the bear, "I don't know. Possibly because it's *all your fault*?"

"That's a bit much," replied the fox. "Blaming the whole thing on a chap like that. It wasn't like I set out to do this. It could have happened to any of us."

"*What* could?" asked Odd, exasperated. "And why can you talk?"

The bear pushed itself up onto all fours. It made a rumbling noise, then it said, "We can talk because, O mortal child—do not be afraid—beneath these animal disguises we wear . . . well, not actual disguises, I mean we *are* actually a bear and a fox and a big bird, which is a rotten sort of thing to happen, but where was I . . . ?"

"Gods!" screeched the eagle.

"Gods?" said Odd.

"Aye. Gods," said the bear. "I was just getting to that. I am great Thor, Lord of the Thunders. The eagle is Lord Odin, All-father, greatest of the Gods. And this runt-eared meddling fox is—"

"Loki," said the fox smoothly. "Blood-brother to the Gods. Smartest, sharpest, most brilliant of all the inhabitants of Asgard, or so they say—"

"Brilliant?" snorted the bear.

"You would have fallen for it. Anyone would," said the fox.

"Fallen for *what*?" said Odd.

A flash of green eyes, a sigh and the fox began. "I'll tell you. And you'll see. It could have happened to anyone. So, Asgard. Home of the mighty. In the middle of a plain, surrounded by an impregnable wall built for us by a Frost Giant. And it was due to me, I should add, that that wall did not cost us the Giant's fee, which was unreasonably high."

"Freya," said the bear. "The Giant wanted Freya. Most lovely of the Goddesses—with, obviously, the exception of Sif, my own little love. And it wanted the Sun and the Moon."

"If you interrupt me one more time," said the fox, *"one more time,* I will not only stop talking, but I shall go off on my own and leave the two of you to fend for yourselves."

The bear said, "Yes, but—"

"Not one word."

31

The bear was silent.

The fox said, "In the great hall of Odin sat all the Gods, drinking mead, eating and telling stories. They drank and bragged and fought and boasted and drank, all through the night and well into the small hours. The women had gone to bed hours since, and now the fires in the hall burned low and most of the Gods slept where they sat, heads resting on the wooden tables. Even great Odin slept in his high chair, his single eye closed in sleep. And yet there was one among the Gods who had drunk and eaten more than any of the others and still was not sleepy. This was I, Loki, called Sky Walker, and I was neither sleepy nor yet drunk, not even a little . . ."

The bear made a noise, a small grumpy harrumph of disbelief. The fox looked at him sharply.

"I said *one word* . . ."

"That wasn't a word," said the bear. "I just made a noise. So. You weren't drunk."

"Right. I wasn't. And not-drunkenly I wandered out from the hall, and I walked, with my shoes that step on air, up to the top of the wall around Asgard, and I looked out over the wall. In the moonlight, standing beneath the wall, staring up at me, I saw the most beautiful woman anyone has ever seen. Her flesh was creamy, her hair was golden, her lips, her shoulders . . . perfection. And in a voice like the striking of a harp string, she called out to me. 'Hail, brave warrior,' she said.

"'Hail yourself,' says I. 'Hail, most beautiful of creatures,' at which she laughed prettily and her eyes sparkled and I knew she liked me. 'And what would a young lady of such loveliness be doing, a-wandering alone, and at night, with wolves and trolls and worse on the loose? Let me offer you hospitality—the hospitality of Loki, mightiest and wisest of all the lords of Asgard. I declare that I shall take you into my own house and care for you in every way that I can!'

"'I cannot accept your offer, O brave and extremely good-looking one,' she said to me, eyes shining like twin sapphires in the moonlight. 'For although you are obviously tall and powerful and extremely attractive, I have promised my father—a king who lives far from here—that I will not give my heart or my lips to any but he who possesses one thing.'

"'And that one thing is?' says I, determined to bring her anything she named.

"'Mjollnir,' says the maiden. 'The Hammer of Thor.'

"Hah! Pausing only to tell her not to go any-where, my feet flew, and like the wind I rushed to the great hall. They were all asleep, or so drunk it made no never mind. There was Thor, sleeping in a drunken stupor, his face on the gravy-covered wooden trencher, and hanging from his side, his hammer. Only the nimble fingers of Loki, wiliest and cleverest, could have teased it from the belt without waking Thor—"

At this, the bear made a deep noise in the back of its throat. After glaring at it for a moment, the fox said, "Heavy it was, that ham-mer. Heavier than people dream. It weighed as much as a small mountain. Too heavy to carry, if you are not Thor. And yet, not too much for my genius. I took off my shoes, which, as I said, can walk on the air, and I tied them, one to the handle and one to the head. Then I snapped my

35

fingers and the hammer followed me.

"This time I hurried to the gates of Asgard. I unbarred them and I walked through—followed, I do not need to tell you, by the hammer.

"The maiden was there. She was sitting on a boulder and she was weeping.

"'Why the tears, O loveliness itself?' I asked.

"At that, she looked up at me with a tear-stained face. 'I weep because once I saw you, great and noble lord, I knew I could never love another. And yet I am doomed to give my heart and my caress only to he who lets me touch the Hammer of Thor.'

"I reached out a hand and touched her cold, wet cheek. 'Dry your tears,' I told her. 'And behold . . . the Hammer of Thor!'

"She stopped crying then, and reached out her delicate hands and held the hammer tightly.

I had reckoned I could have my fun with the lady and still get the hammer back into the hall before Thor woke up. But we would need to get a move on.

"'Now,' I said. 'About that kiss.'

"For a moment I thought she had begun to cry once again, and then I knew that she was laughing. But the noise she made was not a sweet, tinkling, maidenly laugh. It was a deep, crashing noise, like an ice sheet grinding against a mountainside.

"The maiden pulled my shoes from the hammer and dropped them to the ground. She held the hammer as if it was a feather. A wave of cold engulfed me, and I found myself looking up at her, and to make matters worse she wasn't even a *she* any longer.

"She was a man. Well, not a *man*. Male, yes. Yet big as a high hill, icicles hanging from his beard.

37

And she—he, rather—said, 'After so long, all it took was one drunken, lust-ridden oaf, and Asgard is ours.' Then the Frost Giant peered down at me, and he gestured with the Hammer of Thor. 'And you,' he said in a deep and extremely satisfied voice, '*you* need to be something else.'

"I felt my back pushing up. I felt a tail pushing its way out from the base of my spine. My fingers shrank into paws and claws. It wasn't the first time I had turned into animal form—I was a horse once, you know—but it was the first time it was imposed on me from the outside, and it wasn't a nice feeling. Not a nice feeling at all."

"It was worse for us," said the bear. "One moment you are fast asleep, dreaming about thunderstorms, and the next you're being scrunched into a bear. They turned the All-father into an eagle."

The eagle screeched, startling Odd. "Rage!" it said.

"The giant laughed at us, waving my hammer around the while, and then he forced Heimdall to summon the Rainbow Bridge and exiled the three of us here to Midgard. There's no more to tell."

There was silence then in the tiny hut. Only the crackle and spit of a pine branch on the fire.

"Well," said Odd, "Gods or not, I can't keep feeding you, if this winter keeps going. I don't think I can keep feeding me."

"We won't die," said the bear, "because we can't die here. But we'll get hungry. And we'll get more wild. More animal. It's something that happens when you have taken on animal form. Stay in it too long and you become what you pretend to be. When Loki was a horse—"

"We don't talk about that," said the fox.

"So is that why the winter isn't ending?" said Odd.

"The Frost Giants like the winter. They are the winter," said the bear.

"And if spring never comes? If summer doesn't happen? If this winter just goes on forever?"

The bear said nothing. The fox swished its tail impatiently. They looked to the eagle. It tilted its head back, and with one fiery yellow eye it stared at Odd. Then it said, "Death!"

"Eventually," added the fox. "Not immediately. In a year or so. And some creatures will go south. But most of the people and the animals will die. It's happened before, back when we had wars with the Frost Giants at the dawn of time. When they won, huge ice sheets would cover this part of the world. When we won—and if it took us a hundred thousand years, we always did—the ice sheets would retreat and the spring would return. But we were Gods then, not animals."

"And I had my hammer," said the bear.

"Well then," said Odd. "We'll set off as soon as it gets light enough to travel."

"Set off?" said the fox. "For where?"

"Asgard, of course," said Odd, and he smiled his infuriating smile. Then he went back to his little bed, and he went back to sleep.

CHAPTER 4

MAKING RAINBOWS

"WHAT'S THAT YOU'VE GOT there?" asked the fox.

"It's a lump of wood," said Odd. "My father began to carve it into something years ago, and he left it here, but he never came back to finish it."

"What was it going to be?"

"I don't know," admitted Odd. "My father used to say that the carving was in the wood already.

You just had to find out what the wood wanted to be, and then take your knife and remove everything that wasn't that."

"Mm." The fox seemed unimpressed.

Odd was riding on the bear's back. The fox trotted along beside them. High above them, the eagle rode the winds. The sun shone in a cloudless blue sky, and it was colder than it had been when there was cloud cover. They were heading towards higher ground, along a rocky ridge, following a frozen river. The wind hurt Odd's face and ears.

"This won't work," said the bear gloomily. "I mean, whatever it is, it won't."

Odd said nothing.

"You're smiling, aren't you," said the bear. "I can tell."

The thing was this: You got to Asgard, the place

High above them, the eagle rode the winds.

the Gods came from, by crossing the Rainbow Bridge, which was called Bifrost. If you were a God, you simply wiggled your fingers and a rainbow appeared, and you walked across it.

Easy, or so the fox said, and the bear morosely agreed. Or at least, it *was* easy until you didn't have fingers. Which they didn't. Still, even if you didn't have fingers, Loki pointed out, you could normally still find a rainbow and use it. Rainbows turned up after it rained, didn't they?

Well, they didn't in midwinter.

Odd thought about it. He thought about the way rainbows appeared on rainy days, when the sun came out.

"I think," said the bear, "as a responsible adult, I should point a few things out."

"Talk is free," said Odd, "but the wise man chooses when to spend his words." It was

45

something his father used to say.

"I just thought I should point out that we are wasting our time. We don't have any way of getting to the Rainbow Bridge. And if by some miracle we crossed it, look at us—we're animals, and you can barely walk. We can't defeat Frost Giants. This whole thing is hopeless."

"He's right," said the fox.

"If it's hopeless," said Odd, "why are you coming with me?"

The animals said nothing. The morning sun sparkled up at them from the snow, dazzling Odd, making him squint.

"Nothing better to do," said the bear after a while.

"Up here!" said Odd. He clung tightly to the bear's fur as they clambered up the side of a steep hill. They could see the mountains beyond.

46

"Stop," said Odd. The waterfall was one of his favorite places in the world. From spring until midwinter it ran high and fast before it crashed down almost a hundred feet into the valley beneath, where it had carved out a rocky basin. In high summer, when the sun barely set, the villagers would come out to the waterfall and splash around in the basin pool, letting the water tumble onto their heads.

Now, the waterfall was frozen and ice ran from the crags down to the basin in twisted ropes and great clear icicles.

"It's a waterfall," said Odd. "We used to come out here. And when the water came down and the sun was shining brightly, you could see a rainbow, like a huge circle, all around the waterfall."

"No water," said the fox. "No water, no rainbow."

47

"There's water," said Odd. "But it's ice."

He took the axe from his belt, pushed his crutch beneath his arm as he got down from the bear's back and walked over the ice until he stood before the frozen waterfall. He used the crutch to hold himself in position as best he could. Then he began to swing the axe. The noise of the blade hitting the thick icicle cracked off the hills around them, making echoes that sounded as if an entire army of men was hammering on the ice . . .

There was a crash, and an icicle as large as Odd smashed down to the surface of the frozen pool.

"Clever," said the bear, in the kind of tone of voice that meant that it wasn't clever at all. "You broke it."

"Yes," said Odd. He inspected the shards of ice on the ground, picked up the biggest, most cleanly broken piece he could find, then took it to the side of the frozen pool, and put it on a rock, and stared at it.

"It's a lump of ice," said the fox. "If you ask me."

"Yes," said Odd. "I think the rainbows are imprisoned in the ice when the water freezes."

The boy took out his knife and began to trace outlines on the ice block with the blade, going back and forth with it, scoring it as best he could.

The eagle circled high above them, almost invisible in the midwinter sun.

"He's been up there a long time," said the bear. "Do you think he's looking for something?"

The fox said, "I worry about him. It must be hard to be an eagle. He could get lost in there. When I was a horse . . ."

"A mare, you mean," said the bear with a grunt.

The fox tossed its head and walked away. Odd put his knife down and took out his axe once more. "I've seen rainbows on the snow some-times," said Odd, loud enough for the fox to hear, "and on the side of buildings, when the sun shone through the icicles. And I thought, Ice is only water, so it must have rainbows in it too. When the water freezes, the rainbows are trapped in it, like fish in a shallow pool. And the sunlight sets them free."

Odd knelt on the frozen pond. He hit the big lump of ice with his axe. This did nothing—the axe just glanced off the ice and nearly cut into his leg.

"Do that again and you'll break the axe," said the fox. "Hold on."

He nosed along the bank of the frozen pool for several minutes. Then he began scrabbling at the snow. "Here," he said. "This is what you need." He put his paw on a grey rock he had revealed.

Odd pulled at the stone, which came up easily from the ground, and it proved to be a flint. Part of it was grey, but the other part, the translucent part of the flint, was a deep salmon-pink color, and it seemed to have been chipped.

"Don't touch the edges," said the fox. "It'll be sharp. Really sharp. They didn't mess about when they made those things, and they don't blunt easily if you make them well."

"What is it?"

"A hand axe. They used to do sacrifices here, on that big rock over there, and they used tools like this to slice up the animal and to part the

51

flesh from the bones."

"How do you know?" asked Odd.

There was satisfaction and pride in the fox's voice as it said, "Who do you think they were making sacrifices to?"

Odd brought the tool over to the lump of ice. He ran his hands over the ice, slippery as a fish, then he began to attack the ice with the flint. The rock felt warm in his hands. Hot, even.

"It's hot," said Odd.

"Is it?" said the fox, sounding pleased with itself.

The ice fell away under the flint axe, just as Odd had wanted it to. He hacked it into a shape that was almost triangular, thicker on one side than on the other.

The fox and the bear stood nearby watching. The eagle descended to see what was going on, landed in the leafless branches of a tree and was still as a statue.

Odd took his ice triangle and placed it so that the sunlight shone through it onto the white snow that drifted on the frozen pool. Nothing happened. He twisted it, tilted it, moved it around and . . .

A puddle of light appeared on the snow, all the colors of the rainbow . . .

"How is that?" asked Odd.

"But it's on the ground," said the bear doubtfully. "It should be in the air. I mean, how can *that* be a bridge?"

The eagle took off from the tree with a clap of wings, and began to fly upwards.

"I don't think he's very impressed," said the fox. "Nice try."

Odd shrugged. He could feel his mouth pulling

up into a smile even as his heart sank. He had been so proud of himself, making a rainbow. His hands were numb. He hefted the stone axe, was about to throw it, hard, away from him and then simply dropped it.

A screech. Odd looked up to see the eagle plummeting towards them. He began to step back, marvelling at the eagle's speed, wondering how the bird could pull out in time . . .

It didn't pull out.

The eagle hit the patch of colored light on the white snow without slowing, as if it was diving into a pool of liquid water.

The puddle of color splashed . . . and *opened*.

Scarlet fell softly about them and everything was outlined in greens and blues and the world was raspberry-colored and leaf-colored and golden-colored and fire-colored and blueberry-colored and wine-colored. Odd's world was colors, and, despite his crutch, he could feel himself falling forward, tumbling into the rainbow . . .

Everything went dark. Odd's eyes took moments to adjust, and when they did, above him was a velvet night sky, hung with a billion stars. A rainbow arced across it, and Odd was walking on the rainbow—no, not walking: his feet did not move. It felt as if he was being carried up the arch, going upwards, forwards, uncertain how fast he was travelling, only certain that he was somehow swept up in the colors and that it was the colors of the rainbow that were carrying him along.

He looked behind him, wondering if he would see the snowy world he had left, but he saw nothing but blackness, empty even of stars.

Odd's stomach gave a sort of a lurch. He could

feel himself dropping, and he turned his head to
see the rainbow fading. Through the prism of colors he saw huge fir trees, foggy and purple and
blue and red, and then the trees came into focus
and found their own color—a cool bluish green—
as Odd tumbled off the side of a fir tree and down
into a drift of snow. The scent of bruised fir tree
surrounded him.

It was daylight. He was wet, and cold, but
unhurt.

He glanced up, but there was no sign of the
Rainbow Bridge. Silently, across the thick snow,
the fox and the bear were walking towards him.
And then, with a rattle and a clatter, the eagle
landed on a branch beside him, making the snow
on the branch fall *flump* to the ground. The eagle
looked less crazy now, thought Odd. And then, *it
looks bigger.*

"Where is this place?" asked Odd, but he knew the answer, knew it even before the eagle threw back its head and screamed, with delight and with relish and with keen, dark joy, "Asgard!"

CHAPTER 5

AT MIMIR'S WELL

REALLY, TRULY, WITH ALL of his heart, Odd
found that he wanted to believe that he was
still in the world he had known all his life. That
he was still in the country of the Norse folk,
that he was in Midgard. Only he wasn't, and he
knew it. The world smelled different, for a start.
It smelled *alive*. Everything he looked at looked
sharper, more real, more *there*.

And if there was any doubt, then he only had to look at the animals.

"You got bigger," he told them. "You've grown."

And they had. The fox's ears were now level with Odd's chest. The eagle's wingspan, when the bird preened in the sunshine, was as wide as a longship. The bear, which had not been small to begin with, was now the size of Odd's father's hut, enormous in its bulk and in its bearishness.

"We didn't grow," said the fox, its fur the vivid orange color of a blazing fire. "This is how big we are here. We're normal-sized."

Odd nodded. Then he said, "So this whole place is called Asgard, and the town we have to go to is also called Asgard, yes?"

"We named it after ourselves," said the bear. "After the Aesir."

"How far is it to your place?"

The fox sniffed the air, then it looked around. There were mountains behind them, and a forest all about them. "A day's travel. Maybe a little more. Once we get through this forest we reach the plain, and the town is in the center of the plain."

Odd nodded. "I suppose we should get on with it, then."

"There will be time," said the bear. "Asgard is not going anywhere. And right now, I am hungry. I am going fishing. Why don't you two build us a fire?" And without waiting to see what would happen, the great beast lumbered off into the darkness of the forest. The eagle flapped its wings, loud as a small thunderclap, and it took off, circling higher and higher, and then followed the bear.

Odd and the fox gathered wood, finding dry twigs and dead branches, then Odd heaped them high. He took out his knife and sliced a point on a hard stick, put the point against a piece of dry, soft wood, preparing to rotate the stick between his hands, to use the friction to make a fire.

The fox eyed him, unimpressed. "Why bother?" it said. "This is easier." It put its muzzle against the heap of wood, breathed on the twigs. The air above the twigs wavered and shimmered, then, with a crackle, the sticks caught fire.

"How did you do that?"

"This is Asgard," said the fox. "It's less . . . solid . . . than the place you come from. The Gods— even transformed Gods—well, there is power in this place . . . you understand?"

"Not really. But not to worry."

Odd sat beside the fire and he waited for the

bear and the eagle to return. While he waited, he took out the piece of wood his father had started to carve. He inspected it, puzzling over the shape, familiar yet strange, wondering what it had been intended to be, and why it should bother him so. He ran his thumb over it, and it comforted him.

It was twilight by the time the bear brought back the largest trout Odd had ever seen. The boy gutted it with his knife (the fox devoured the raw guts enthusiastically), then he speared it through with a long stick, cut two forked sticks to make an improvised spit and he roasted it over the fire, turning it every few minutes to ensure it did not burn.

When the fish was cooked, the eagle took the head, and the other three divided the meat between them, the bear eating more than the other two put together.

The twilight edged imperceptibly into night, and a huge, dark-yellow moon began to rise on the horizon, achingly slowly.

When they had finished eating, the fox went to sleep beside the fire, and the eagle flapped heavily off into a dead pine to sleep. Odd took the leftover fish and pushed it into a drift of snow, to keep it fresh, as his mother had taught him.

The bear looked at Odd. Then it said casually, "You must be thirsty. Come on. Let's look for some water."

Odd climbed onto the bear's broad back, and held tight as it lumbered off into the darkness of the forest.

It didn't feel like they were looking for anything, though. It felt like the bear knew exactly where he was going, that he was heading somewhere. Up a

ridge and down into a small gorge and through a
copse of trees, magical in its stillness, and then
they were pushing through scratchy gorse, and
now they were in a small clearing, in the center
of which was a pool of liquid water.

"Careful," said the bear, quietly. "It goes down
a long way."

Odd stared. The yellow moonlight was decep-
tive, but still . . .

"There are shapes moving in the water," he
said.

"Nothing in there that will hurt you," said the
bear. "They're just reflections, really. It's safe to
drink. I give you my word."

Odd untied his wooden cup from his belt. He
dipped it into the water, and he drank. The water
was refreshing and strangely sweet. He had not
realized how thirsty he had been, and he filled

and emptied his wooden cup four times.

And then he yawned. "Feel so sleepy."

"It's all the travelling," said the bear. "Here. Let me." It pulled over several fallen fir branches at the edge of the clearing with its teeth. "Curl up on these."

"But the others . . ." said Odd.

"I'll tell them you fell asleep in the woods," said the bear. "Just don't go wandering off. For now, just rest."

And the bear lay down on the branches, crushing them under its bulk. The boy lay beside the animal, smelling the deep bearish scent of it, pushing against the fur and feeling the softness and the warmth.

The world was comfortable and quiet and warm. He was safe, and everything was enclosed by the dark . . .

When he opened his eyes once more, he was cold, and he was alone, and the moon was huge and white and high in the sky. *More than twice as big as the moon in Midgard,* thought Odd, and he wondered if that was because Asgard was closer to the moon, or whether it had its own moon . . .

The bear was gone.

In the pale moonlight Odd could see shapes moving in the water of the pool, and he pulled himself to his feet and limped over to look more closely.

At the water's edge he crouched down, made a cup from his hand, scooped up water, and drank. The water was icy cold, but as he drank he felt warmed and safe and comfortable.

The figures in the water dissolved and re-formed.

66

"What do you need to see?" asked a voice from behind Odd.

Odd said nothing.

"You have drunk from my spring," said the voice.

"Did I do something wrong?" asked Odd.

There was silence. Then, "No," said the voice. It sounded very old, so ancient Odd could not tell if it was a man's voice or a woman's. Then the voice said, "Look."

On the water's surface he saw reflections. His father, in the winter, playing with him and his mother—a silly game of blindman's buff that left them all giggling and helpless on the ground . . .

He saw a huge creature, with icicles in its beard and hair like the pattern the frost makes on the leaves and on the ice early in the morning, sitting beside a huge wall, scanning the horizon rest-lessly.

He saw his mother sitting in a corner of the great hall, sewing up Fat Elfred's worn jerkin, and her eyes were red with tears.

He saw the cold plains where the Frost Giants live, saw Frost Giants hauling rocks, and feasting on great horned elk, and dancing beneath the moon.

He saw his father, sitting in the woodcutter's hut he had so recently left himself. His father had a knife in one hand, a lump of wood in the other. He began to carve, a strange, distant smile on his face. Odd knew that smile . . .

He saw his father as a young man, leaping from the longship into the sea and running up a craggy beach. Odd knew that this was Scotland, that soon his father would meet his mother . . .

He saw his mother sitting in a corner of the great hall . . .
and her eyes were red with tears.

He kept watching.

The moonlight was so bright in that place. Odd could see what he needed to. After some time, he pulled out the lump of wood he had found in his father's hut and his knife, and he began to carve, in smooth, confident strokes, removing everything that wasn't part of the carving.

He carved until daybreak, when the bear crunched through the trees into the clearing.

It did not ask what Odd had seen in the pool, and Odd did not volunteer anything.

Odd climbed onto the bear's back. "You're getting smaller again," said Odd. This was no longer the huge bear of the previous evening. Now it seemed only slightly bigger than it had been the first time Odd had ridden it. "You've shrunk."

"If you say so," said the bear.

"Where do the Frost Giants come from?" asked

Odd, as they bounded through the forest.

"Jotunheim," said the bear. "It means *giants' home*. It's across the great river. Mostly they stay on their own side. But they've crossed before. One time, one of them wanted the Sun, the Moon and Lady Freya. The time before that, they wanted my hammer, Mjollnir, and the hand of Lady Freya. There was one time they wanted all the treasures of Asgard and Lady Freya . . ."

"They must like Lady Freya a lot," said Odd.

"They do. She's very pretty."

"What's it like in Jotunheim?" asked Odd.

"Bleak. Treeless. Cold. Desolate. Nothing like it is here. You should ask Loki."

"Why?"

"He wasn't always one of the Aesir. He was born a Frost Giant. He was the smallest Frost Giant ever. They used to laugh at him. So he left.

Saved Odin's life, on his travels. And he . . ." The bear hesitated and seemed to think twice about whatever he had been going to say, then finished, ". . . he keeps things interesting." And then the bear said, "Anything that you did last night, anything you saw . . ."

"Yes?"

"The wise man knows when to keep silent. Only the fool tells all he knows."

The fox and the eagle were waiting beside the remains of the fire. Odd finished what was left of the fish. Then the bear said, "Well? What do we do now?"

Odd said, "Take me to the edge of the forest. You wait for me. I'll walk alone from there to the gates of Asgard."

"Why?" asked the fox.

"Because I don't want the Frost Giants knowing

you three are back," said Odd. "Not yet."

They set off.

"I could get very used to travelling by bear," Odd said. But the bear only grunted.

CHAPTER 6

THE GATES OF ASGARD

WHERE THE FOREST ENDED, the bear stopped, and Odd climbed off. He put his crutch beneath his armpit, gripped it hard with his right hand.

"Right," he said. "Wish me good luck. The blessing of the Gods must count for something."

"What if you don't come back?" said the fox.

"Then you're no worse off now than you were before you met me," said Odd cheerfully. "Anyway, why shouldn't I come back?"

"They could eat you," said the bear.

Odd blinked. "Ah . . . *do* Frost Giants eat people?"

There was a pause. The fox said, "Occasionally" at the same time as the bear said, "Almost never."

The fox coughed. "I wouldn't worry," it said. "There's barely any meat on you. You'd scarcely be worth the trouble of eating." It grinned. This did nothing to make Odd feel any better. He hefted his crutch and began to walk, slowly, laboriously, towards the huge stone wall that surrounded the city of the Gods.

The snow had blown clear of the path, and although the ground was slippery in places, he found the walk was not as hard as he had expected.

Days were longer here in Asgard. The sun was a silver coin that hung in the white sky. Odd pushed himself to keep walking, one step at a time, remembering back when he had walked with ease and never thought twice about the miracle of putting one foot in front of the other and pushing the world towards you.

At first, Odd thought that the wall of Asgard was as high as a tall man and that there was a pale statue of a man sitting on a boulder beside it—at least, he imagined it to be a statue. And then he moved slowly closer, and closer, and the wall grew, and the pale statue grew also, until, as the boy got closer still, he had to throw back his head to look at them.

Every step he took towards the gates, towards

the huge pale figure on the boulder, he felt the temperature drop.

And then the statue moved, and Odd knew.

"WHO ARE YOU?" The voice tumbled across the plain like an avalanche.

"I'm called Odd," shouted Odd, and he smiled.

The Frost Giant peered down at him. There were icicles in its eyebrows, and its eyes were the color of lake ice just before it cracks and drops you into freezing water.

"WHAT ARE YOU? A GOD? A TROLL? SOME KIND OF WALKING CORPSE?"

"I'm a boy," yelled Odd, and he smiled again.

"AND WHAT IN YMIR'S NAME ARE YOU DOING *HERE*?"

It is a strange sensation, talking to a being who could crush you like a man could crush a baby mouse. *And*, thought Odd, *at least mice can run.*

"I'm here to drive the Frost Giants from Asgard," explained Odd. Then he smiled at the giant, a big, happy, irritating smile.

It was the smile that did it. If Odd had not smiled, the giant would simply have picked him up and crushed the life from him, or squashed him against the boulder, or bitten his head off and kept him to snack on later. But that smile, a smile that said that Odd knew more than he was saying . . .

"No, you won't," said the Frost Giant. "You can't."

"'Fraid so," said Odd.

"I outwitted Loki," said the Frost Giant portentously. "I bested Thor. I banished Odin. All of Asgard is pacified and under my rule. Even now, my brothers march from Jotunheim, as reinforcements." He darted a look towards the horizon, to the north. "The Gods are my slaves. I am betrothed to the lovely Freya. And you honestly think you can go up against me?"

Odd just shrugged and continued to smile. It was his broadest, most irritating smile, and at home, it had always gotten him hit. Even the giant wanted to hurt him, to wipe that smile off his face. But nobody had smiled at the giant like that before, and it bothered him.

"I rule Asgard!" boomed the giant.

"Why?" asked Odd.

"WHY?"

"I can hear you fine without you shouting," said Odd, when the reverberations had died away. And then he said, pitching his voice just a little quieter, so the giant had to lean in to listen, "Why do you want to rule Asgard? Why did you take it over?"

79

The frost giant raised himself from the huge boulder. Then he jerked a thumb behind him. "See that wall?" he said.

You couldn't avoid seeing it. It filled the world. Every stone in the wall was bigger than the houses in Odd's village.

"My brother built that wall. He made a deal with the Gods—to build them a wall inside six months, or he would take no payment. And on the last day, as he was just about to complete it . . . on the *last* hour of the *last* day, they cheated him."

"How?"

"A mare, the most beautiful animal anyone had ever seen, ran across the plain and lured away the stallion who was hauling the stones for my brother. It used womanish wiles. The stallion broke its bonds, and the horses ran off into the woods together and were gone. And then, just when my poor brother had nerved himself up to complain about how he was being treated, Thor returned from his travels and killed him with his damnable hammer. That's how every tale of the Gods and the Frost Giants ends—with Thor killing Giants. Well, not this time."

"Obviously not," said Odd, who was beginning to have his suspicions about who the mare had been. "So, what did your brother want for payment?"

"Nothing really," said the giant, shifting from foot to foot. "Just stuff."

He sat down again on the boulder. Where the air touched the Frost Giant, it seemed to steam. Odd had seen the water in the fjord steam in winter, when the air was colder than the water. He wondered how cold the Frost Giant was.

"He wanted the Sun," said the giant, "the Moon. And Freya. All things that I now control, for Asgard is mine!"

"Yes. You said that."

There was a pause. The Frost Giant looked tired, Odd thought. Then Odd said, again, "Why? Why did he want those things?"

The Frost Giant took a deep breath. "HOW DARE YOU QUESTION ME!" he roared, and Odd felt the earth shake beneath him. He leaned on his crutch to keep his balance as icy winds blew past him. Odd didn't say anything. He just smiled some more.

The giant said, "Would you mind if I picked you up? It would make it easier to talk if we were face-to-face."

"So long as you're careful," said Odd.

The giant reached down and laid his hand flat

on the ground, palm up, and Odd clambered awkwardly onto it. Then the giant cupped his hand and lifted Odd up, so the boy was on a level with his mouth, and the giant whispered, in a voice like the howl of a winter wind, "Beauty."

"Beauty?"

"The three most beautiful things there are. The Sun, the Moon and Freya the lovely. It's not beautiful, really, in Jotunheim. There's just rocks and crags and . . . Well, they can be beautiful too, if you take them the right way. And we can see the Sun there, and the Moon. No Freya—nothing that beautiful. She's beautiful. But she does have a tongue on her."

"So you came here for beauty?"

"Beauty, and revenge for my brother. I told the other Frost Giants I'd do it, and they all laughed at me. But they aren't laughing now, are they?"

83

Then the giant cupped his hand and lifted Odd up,
so the boy was on a level with his mouth.

"What about spring?"

"Spring?"

"Spring. In Midgard. Where I come from. It isn't happening this year. And if the winter continues, then everyone will die. People. Animals. Plants."

Frosty blue eyes bigger than windows stared at Odd. "Why should I care about that?" The Frost Giant put Odd down on the top of the wall around Asgard, the wall his brother had built. It was windy up there, and Odd leaned into his crutch, scared that a gust of wind would blow him away and down to his death. He glanced behind him, and was not surprised to see that the home of the Gods looked almost exactly like the village on the fjord from which he had come. Bigger, of course, but of the same pattern—a feasting hall and smaller buildings all around it.

Odd said, "You should care because you care about beauty. And there won't be any. There will just be dead things."

"Dead things can be beautiful," said the Frost Giant. "Anyway, I won it. I beat them. I fooled them and I tricked them. I banished Thor and Odin and that miniature turncoat Loki." And then he sighed.

Odd remembered what he had seen in the pool, the previous night. He said, "Do you really think your brothers are on the way?"

"Ah," said the Frost Giant. "Um. They may be. I mean, they all said they would . . . if I did . . . It's just that I don't think that any of them actually *expected* me to conquer this place, and they all have things to do, farms and houses and children and wives. I don't think that they really *want* to come down to the hot lands and play soldiers guarding a bunch of grumpy Gods."

"And I suppose they can't *all* be betrothed to lovely Freya."

"Lucky them," said the Frost Giant, darkly. "She's beautiful. Oh yes. She's beautiful. I'll give you that." He shook his head. Icicles fell from his hair and crashed, tinkling, on the rocks beneath. "She's got a carriage pulled by cats, you know. I tried stroking them." He held up the index finger of his right hand. It was covered in scratches and cuts. "She said it was my own fault. That I'd got them overexcited.

"She *is* beautiful," he said, and sighed. "But she only comes up to the top of my foot. She shouts louder than a giantess when she's angry. And she's always angry."

"But you can't go home when you've won," said Odd.

"Exactly. You wait here, in this hot, horrible place, for reinforcements who don't want to come, while the locals hate you . . ."

"So go home," said Odd. "Tell them that I beat you." He wasn't smiling now.

The Frost Giant looked at Odd, and Odd looked at the Frost Giant.

The Frost Giant said, "You're too small to fight. You would have to have outwitted me."

Odd nodded. "My mother used to tell me stories about boys who tricked giants. In one of them, they had a stone-throwing contest, but the boy had a bird, not a stone, and it went up into the air and just kept going."

"I'd never fall for that one," said the giant. "Anyway, birds, they just head for the nearest tree."

"I am trying," said Odd, "to allow you to go home with your honor intact and a whole skin.

You aren't making it any easier for me."

The giant said, "A whole skin?"

"You banished Thor to Midgard," said Odd, "yet he's back now. It's only a matter of time until he gets here."

The giant blinked. "But I have his hammer," he said. "I turned it into this boulder I sit on."

"Go home."

"But if I take Freya back to Jotunheim, she'll just shout at me and make everything worse. And if I take Thor's hammer, he'll just come after it, and one day he'll get it, and *then* he'll kill me."

Odd nodded in agreement. It was true. He knew it was.

When, in the years that followed, the Gods told this tale, late at night, in their great hall, they always hesitated at this point, because in a moment Odd will reach into his jerkin and pull out something carved of wood, and none of them, try how they might, was certain what it was.

Some of the Gods claimed that it was a wooden key, and some said it was a heart. There was a school of thought that maintained that what Odd had presented the giant with was a realistic carving of Thor's hammer, and that the giant had been unable to tell the real from the false, and had fled, in terror.

It was none of these things.

Before he took it out, Odd said, "My father met my mother when our village was raiding somewhere in Scotland. That's far to the south of us. He discovered her trying to hide her father's sheep in a cave, and she was the most beautiful thing he had ever seen. So he brought her, and the sheep, home. He would not even touch her until he had taught her enough of the way we speak to be able to tell her he wanted her for his wife. But he said that on the voyage home, she was so beautiful she lit up the world. And she did. She lit up his world, like the summer sun."

"This was before you were born," said the Frost Giant.

"True," said Odd, "but I saw it."

"How?"

Odd knew, without being told, that it would be very, very wrong to mention the pool in the forest to the Frost Giant, let alone the shapes that he had seen moving in the pool the night before. He lied, but it was the truth also. He said, "I saw it in my father's eyes. He loved her, and a few years ago he started to make something for her, but he left it unfinished, and then he didn't come back to finish it. So last night, I finished it for him. At first I didn't know how it was meant to look, and then I saw her . . . I mean, it's as I imagine her, my mother, when they had just met. Stolen from her people and her land, but brave and determined, and not ever going to give in to fear or grief or loneliness."

The giant said nothing.

Odd said, "You came here for beauty, didn't you? And you can't go back empty-handed."

He reached into his jerkin and he took out the thing that he had carved. His father's carving, which he had finished. It was his mother, as she had looked before he was born. It was the finest thing that Odd had ever made, and it was beautiful.

The Frost Giant squinted at it, and then, just for a moment, smiled. He put the carved head into his pouch, and he said, "It is . . . remarkable. And lovely. Yes. I will take it back with me to Jotunheim, and it will brighten my hall." The Frost Giant hesitated, then he said, a little wistfully, "Do you think I should say good-bye to Lady Freya?"

Odd said, "If you do, she'll probably shout at you some more."

"Or beg me to take her with me," said the Frost Giant. Odd could have sworn that the Frost Giant shivered at that.

The Frost Giant took a step away from Odd, and as he moved away, he grew. He went from being the size of a high hill to being the size of a mountain. Then he reached an arm up into the grey of the winter sky. His hand vanished in the cloud . . .

"I think I need good weather to leave in," said the giant. "Something to hide my tracks and to make me hard to follow."

93

Odd could not see quite what the Frost Giant did, but when he lowered his hand, snow began to fall in huge white flakes that spun and tumbled and obscured the world. The giant began to lumber away into the blizzard.

"Hey!" called Odd. "I don't know your name!"

But the figure did not hear him, or if it did, it did not answer, and in moments it was lost to sight.

CHAPTER 7

FOUR TRANSFORMATIONS AND A MEAL

THE EAGLE FOUND HIM, as he sat on the wall, in an area that he had kept as free of snow as he could. The great bird landed beside the boy.

"Good?" it said. It was twilight, and the snow was falling more gently now.

"I'm cold," said Odd. "I nearly got blown off there a couple of times. I was getting worried I'd have to spend the rest of my life up on this wall.

95

The great bird landed beside the boy.

But, yes, I'm good."

The eagle simply looked at him.

"The Frost Giant's gone," said Odd. "I made him go away."

"How?" asked the eagle.

"Magic," said Odd, and he smiled, and thought, *If magic means letting things do what they wanted to do, or be what they wanted to be . . .*

"Down," said the eagle.

Odd eyed the snowy rocks that made the wall. "I can't climb down that," he said. "I'll die."

The eagle launched itself from the edge of the wall, circled downward. It soon returned, flapping heavily, carrying a worn-looking soft leather shoe, which it dropped on the wall beside Odd. Off again it went, into the snowy dusk, and came back with a shoe that was a twin to the first.

"They're too big for me," said Odd.

97

"Loki's," said the eagle.

"Oh," said Odd, remembering the shoes from Loki's story, the ones that walked in the sky. He pulled them on. Then, warily, heart pounding, Odd limped to the edge of the wall, and when he got to the edge, he stopped.

He tried to jump, and nothing happened. He didn't move a muscle.

Oh come on, he told his feet, his good one and the one that was broken and twisted, the one that hurt all the time. *You've got magical flying shoes on. Just walk out into the air, and you'll be fine.*

But his feet and his legs ignored him, and he stood where he was. He turned to the eagle, who was wheeling above Odd's head impatiently. "I can't do it," he said. "I've tried and I can't."

The eagle gave a screech, flapped its wings

hard, and rose into the snowy air.

Another screech. Odd looked around. The eagle was heading straight for him, wings outstretched, hooked beak open wide, talons out, single eye aflame . . .

Odd took an involuntary step backwards, and the eagle's claws missed him by less than the width of a feather . . .

"What was *that* for?" he shouted after the bird.

Then he looked down and saw the ground that wasn't under his feet. He was a very long way up, standing unsupported on the air.

"Oh," said Odd. Then he smiled, and he slid down the sky like a boy going down a hill, shouting as he did so something that sounded remarkably like "Whee!" and he landed as lightly as a snowflake.

Odd pushed himself back up into the air and began to jump, ten, twenty, thirty feet at a time . . .

He moved towards the cluster of wooden buildings that were Asgard, and did not stop until he heard the sound of cats, mewing and *mrow*ling . . .

The Goddess Freya was nowhere near as scary as Odd had imagined from the Frost Giant's description. True, she was beautiful, and her hair was golden, and her eyes were the blue of the summer sky, but it was her smile that Odd warmed to— amused, and gentle, and forgiving. It was safe, that smile, and he told her everything, or almost.

When she understood who the three animals really were, her smile became wider.

"Well, well, well," she said. And then she said, "Boys!" They were in the great mead hall now. It was empty and no fire burned in the hearth.

The Goddess reached out her right arm.

The eagle, which had been sitting on the ornately carved back of the highest chair, flapped over and landed awkwardly on her wrist. Its talons gripped her pale flesh so hard that crimson beads of blood welled up, yet she did not appear to notice this, or to be in any visible discomfort.

She scratched the back of the bird's neck with her fingernail, and it preened against her.

"Odin All-father," she said. "Wisest of the Aesir. One-eyed Battle God. You who drank the water of wisdom from Mimir's Well . . . return to us." And then, with her left hand, she began to reshape the bird, to push at it, to change it . . .

A tall, grey-bearded man, with a cruel, wise face stood before them. He was naked, something he seemed scarcely to notice. He walked over to the tall chair, picked up a large grey cloak, and an ancient floppy-brimmed hat—which Odd could have sworn had not been there the last time he looked—and he put them on.

"I was far away," he told Freya absently. "And getting farther away with every moment that passed. Good job."

But Freya had already put her attention on the bear, and was kneading at it with both hands, pushing and shaping, like a mother bear licking her cubs into shape. Beneath her fair hands the bear changed. He was red-bearded and covered in hair, and his upper arms looked as knotted and as powerful as ancient trees. He was the biggest man, who was not a giant, that Odd had ever seen. He looked friendly, and he winked at Odd, which made the boy feel strangely proud.

Odin tossed Thor a tunic, and he walked into

the shadows to get dressed. Then he paused, and turned back.

"I need my hammer," Thor said. "I need Mjollnir."

"I know where it is," said Odd. "It was hidden as a boulder. I can show you, if you like."

"When we've finished the important business at hand, perhaps?" said the fox. "Me next."

Freya looked at the animal, amused. "You know," she said, "many people will find you much easier to cope with in that shape. Are you sure you don't want me to leave you?"

The fox growled, then the growl became a choked cough, and the fox said, "Fair Freya, you joke with me. But do not the bards sing:

"'*A woman both fair and just and compassionate*
"'*Only she can be compared to glorious Freya'?*"

"Loki, you caused all this," she said. "*All* of it."

"Yes," he said. "I admit it. But I found the boy as well. You can't just focus on the bad stuff."

"One day," said Freya softly, "I will regret this." But she smiled to herself, and she reached a hand out and touched the black tip of the fox's muzzle, then ran her finger up between its ears and along its spine and all the way up to the very tip of its tail.

A shimmer—then a man stood in front of them, beardless, flame-haired, as pale of skin as Freya herself. Eyes like green chips of ice. Odd wondered if Loki had a fox's eyes still, or if the fox had always had Loki's eyes.

Thor threw Loki some clothes. "Cover your-self," he said bluntly.

Now Freya turned her attention to Odd. Her gentle smile filled his world. "Your turn," she said.

"I look like this anyway," said Odd.

"I know," said Freya. She knelt down beside him, reached out a hand towards his injured leg. "May I?"

"Um. If you want to."

She picked him up as if he was light as a leaf, and put him down on the great feasting table of the Gods. She reached down to his right foot and deftly unhooked it at the knee. She ran a nail across the shin and the flesh parted. Freya looked at the bone, and her face fell. "It was crushed," she said, "so much that not even I can repair it.' And then she said, "But I can help."

She pushed her hand into the inside of Odd's leg, kneading the smashed bones, pulling together the fragments from inside the leg, smoothing them together. Then she opened the flesh of the foot and repeated the same operation, putting the pieces of foot bone and toe bone back where they were meant to be. And then she encased the skeletal leg and foot in flesh once more, sealed it up, and the Goddess Freya reattached Odd's leg to Odd, and it was as if it had always been there.

"Sorry," she said. "I did the best I could do. It's better, but it's not right, yet." She seemed lost in thought, then she said brightly, "Why don't I replace it entirely? What about a cat's rear leg? Or a chicken's?"

Odd smiled, and shook his head. "My leg is fine," he said.

Odd stood up cautiously, put his weight on his right leg, trying to pretend he had not just seen his leg unhooked at the knee. It did not hurt. Not really. Not like it used to.

"Give it time," said Freya.

A huge hand came down and clapped Odd on

the shoulder, sending him flying.

"Now, laddie," boomed Thor. "Tell us just how you defeated the might of the Frost Giants." He seemed much more cheerful than when he had been a bear.

"There was only one of them," said Odd.

"When *I* tell the story," said Thor, "there will be at least a dozen."

"I want my shoes back," said Loki.

There was a feast that night in the great mead hall of the Gods. Odin sat at the end of the table, in the magnificent, carved chair, saying almost as little as he had when he was an eagle. Thor, on his left side, boomed enthusiastically. Loki, who had to sit down at the far end of the table, was pleasant enough to everyone until he got drunk, and then, like a candle suddenly blowing out, he became unpleasant, and he said mean, foolish, unrepeatable things, and he leered at the Goddesses, and soon enough Thor and a large man with one hand, who Odd thought might have been called Tyr, were carrying Loki from the hall.

"He doesn't learn," said Odd.

He thought he had said it to himself, in his head, but Freya, who was sitting beside him, said, "No. He doesn't learn. None of them do. And they don't change, either. They can't. It's all part of being a God."

Odd nodded. He thought he understood, a little.

Then Freya said, "Have you eaten enough? Have you drunk your fill?"

"Yes, thank you," said Odd.

Old Odin left his chair, and walked towards

them. He wiped the goose grease from his mouth with his sleeve, smearing even more grease all over his grey beard. He said, quietly, into Odd's ear, "Do you know what spring it was you drank from, boy? Where the water came from? Do you know what it cost me to drink there, many years ago? You didn't think you defeated the Frost Giants alone, did you?"

Odd said only, "Thank you."

"No," said Odin. "Thank *you*." The All-father was leaning on a staff carved with faces—dogs and horses and men and birds, skulls and reindeer and mice and women—all of them wrapped around Odin's stick. You could look at it for hours and still not see every detail on that stick. Odin pushed the staff towards Odd and said, "This is for you."

Odd said, "But . . ."

The old God looked at him gravely through his one good eye. "It is never wise to refuse the gifts of the Gods, boy."

Odd said, "Well, thank you." And he took the staff. It was comfortable. It felt as though he could walk a long way, as long as he was leaning on that staff.

Odin dipped his hand into a pitcher, brought it out holding a small globe of water no larger than a man's eyeball. He placed the water ball in front of a candle flame. "Look into this," he said.

Odd looked into the ball of water, and his world became a rainbow, and then it went dark.

When he opened his eyes, he was home.

CHAPTER 8

AFTERWARDS

ODD LEANED HIS WEIGHT on the staff and looked down at the village. Then he began to walk the path that would take him home. He was still limping, a little. His right foot would never be as strong as his left. But it did not hurt, and he was grateful to Freya for that.

As he headed down the path to the village, he heard a rushing noise. It was the sound of snow melting, of new water trying to find its way to lower ground. Sometimes he heard a *clump* as snow fell from a tree onto the ground beneath, sometimes the deep *thrum thrum thrum,* followed by a harsh cracking sound, as the ice that had covered the edge of the bay through this eternal winter began to cleave and to break up.

In a few days, Odd thought, *this will all be mud. In a few weeks it will be a riot of greenery.*

Odd reached the village. For a moment he wondered if he had come to the wrong place, for nothing looked as he remembered it looking when he had left, less than a week before. He remembered how the animals had grown, when they reached Asgard, and then, how they seemed, later, to have shrunk.

He wondered if it was the air of Asgard that

did it, or if it had happened when he drank the water of the pool.

He reached Fat Elfred's door and he rapped upon it sharply with his staff.

"Who is it?" called a voice.

"It's me. Odd," he said.

There was a noise inside the hut, an urgent whispering, then people talking in low voices. Odd could hear the loudest of the voices as it grumbled about good-for-nothings who stole a side of salmon, and how it was high time for someone to be taught a lesson he would never forget. He heard the sound of a door being unbarred.

The door opened and Fat Elfred looked out. He stared at Odd, confused.

"I'm sorry," he said, in a most un-sorry tone of voice. "I thought my runaway stepson was here."

Odd looked down at the man. Then he smiled

and he said, "It is him. I mean, it's me. I'm him. I'm Odd."

Fat Elfred said nothing. The heads of his various sons and daughters appeared around him. They looked up at Odd nervously.

"Is my mother here?" asked Odd.

Fat Elfred coughed. "You grew," he said. "If that *is* you."

Odd just smiled—a smile so irritating that it had to be him.

The smallest of Fat Elfred's children said, "They got into fights after you went away. She said we had to go and look for you and that it was Dad's fault you'd run off, and he said it wasn't and he wouldn't and good riddance to bad rubbish and she said right then, and she went back to your father's old house on the other side of town."

"It is him. I mean, it's me. I'm him. I'm Odd."

Odd winked down at the boy, as Thor had once winked at him, and turned around and, leaning on his carved staff, limped through the village, which already seemed much too small for him and not just because he had grown so much since he had left. Soon the ice would melt and long-ships would be sailing. He did not imagine anyone would refuse him a berth on a ship. Not now that he was big. They would need a good pair of hands on the oars, after all. Nor would they argue if he chose to bring a passenger . . .

He reached down and knocked on the door of the house in which he had been born. And when his mother opened the door, before she could hug him, before she could cry and laugh and cry once more, before she could offer him food and exclaim over how big he had grown and how fast children do spring up when they are out of your sight, before any of these things could happen, Odd said, "Hello, Mother. How would you like to go back to Scotland? For a while, at least."

"That would be a fine thing," she said.

And Odd smiled, and ducked his head to get through the door, and went inside.